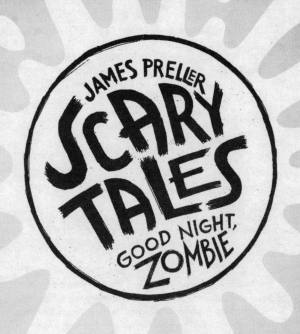

JAMES PRELLER

SCARY TALES

GOOD NIGHT, ZOMBIE

Illustrated by IACOPO BRUNO

MACMILLAN CHILDREN'S BOOKS

First published in the US 2013 by Feiwel and Friends

This edition published in the UK 2013 by Macmillan Children's Books
a division of Macmillan Publishers Limited
20 New Wharf Road, London N1 9RR
Basingstoke and Oxford
Associated companies throughout the world
www.panmacmillan.com

ISBN 978-1-4472-4691-6

35798642

A CIP catalogue record for this book is available from
the British Library.

For Maddie and PJ —
you guys scare me.

CONTENTS

1 TRAPPED 3

2 NO WI-FI 9

3 LIGHTS FLICKER AND DIE 15

4 THE MYSTERIOUS MR
   VAN DER KLEMP 21

5 WALKERS IN THE MIST 25

6 THE FACE AT THE WINDOW 29

7 CARTER GOES FOR HELP 35

8 OOOOOAAAAANNNN,
   OOOOOAAAAANNNN 41

9 'THEY'RE COMING!' 47

10 THE UNDEAD CANNOT BE STOPPED 53

11 'THEY WILL COME' 61

12 AND THEY CAME 67

13 SUNRISE 77

14 STRANGERS AT SCHOOL 81

.... AND THEN

IN THE GATHERING DARK OF AUTUMN TWILIGHT, THREE STUDENTS ENTER A NEAR-EMPTY ELEMENTARY SCHOOL. THEY HUSTLE TO FETCH FORGOTTEN THINGS: BOOKS, ASSIGNMENTS, BASKETBALL TRAINERS.

THEY ARE NOT FRIENDS. THEY SCARCELY KNOW EACH OTHER.

BUT THEY WILL SOON BE TRAPPED INSIDE — DOORS CHAINED, LOCKED SHUT. IN THE BASEMENT, A MYSTERIOUS NIGHT CARETAKER WAITS. AND OUTSIDE, MOVING IN THE MIST, DARK SHAPES SHUFFLE CLOSER, EVER CLOSER . . .

1

TRAPPED

Carter Novack pulled hard on the school front doors. He pushed, tugged again and pounded on the door with the side of his fist. 'What the heck?!'

Thick chains were wrapped around the handles. A heavy padlock sealed the deal. Carter was locked *inside* – trapped in Buzz Aldrin Primary School on a Friday night. He yanked again on the front doors. The clatter echoed in the corridors, bouncing off pale green walls and tiled floors.

A girl in jeans and a North Face jacket stood watching him. Her name was Esme. She was tall and string-bean thin and wore a frown.

Esme cleared her throat. Carter turned his head to look at her. 'What?'

'You'll break it,' Esme said.

'Are you my mother?' Carter asked.

'I . . . what?'

'I asked, "Are you my mother?" Because if you're not, then you can stay out of my business,' Carter said.

Esme's lips tightened to a narrow line. She didn't know Carter, but she knew his type – boys who made rude jokes and interrupted in the classroom.

Carter vibrated with frustration. He suddenly kicked out at the lock, hard, three times: **WHAM, WHAM, WHAM!** The violence frightened Esme Millstein. But it also made her heart quicken, *pitter-pat*. He was very strong.

Footsteps approached from the east wing of the building, coming from the music room. A small, gum-chewing boy named Arnold Chang soon arrived. His baseball cap was screwed on sideways.

Esme knew Arnold from her Year Four class last year. Arnold was very clever, but strange. Most boys were. At least, that's the way Esme figured it.

Now, three Year Five students paused in the main hallway.

'It's locked?' Arnold asked.

Carter shot him a look. 'Ya think, Sherlock?'

'So, we're trapped?' Arnold asked. He looked to Esme.

'I guess,' she mumbled.

'There's got to be another way out,' Carter announced. He stormed off in the direction of the library and the Reception classrooms.

Esme sucked on a strand of hair. 'Do you have a phone?' she asked Arnold.

'At home,' he answered. 'You?'

'I'm not allowed, I mean –' Esme corrected herself, 'I don't have a phone, not at the moment.'

A smile snuck across Arnold's face. 'Not at the moment?' he repeated.

Esme ignored Arnold's tone. 'Where are all the teachers?'

Arnold glanced at the wall clock. 'It's nearly six o'clock on a Friday night. They're probably all home by now.' With a dip of his left shoulder, he let his backpack drop to the floor with a thud. The top part of a skateboard poked out of it. 'I cruised by to get some books,' he said. 'I was surprised the place was even open.'

The sound of rattling chains came from around the corner, followed by a scream.

Arnold didn't wait. He scooped up his backpack, leaped on the skateboard, and pushed off down the hallway.

NO WI-FI

Esme caught up with the boys outside the library.

'Locked!' Carter fumed. The muscles in his neck twitched. 'Every door, it's the same thing. Chains and locks.'

'Chill, dude,' Arnold said, laughing. 'We'll figure it out.'

Esme tried the library door. It opened. 'Don't worry. We can use the phone.'

Carter nodded. Arnold rolled slowly

forward on his skateboard.

'You know those aren't allowed in school,' Esme said. 'Skateboards are against the rules.'

A look of disbelief passed between Arnold and Carter. *Was she for real?* Esme extended a long arm across the doorway, blocking their path.

'Seriously?' Arnold asked.

'This is the library,' Esme whispered with a slight quiver in her voice, as if talking about a sacred place. 'No skateboards.'

Carter ducked under Esme's outstretched arm. But Arnold stood at the threshold, thinking it over. He finally said, 'I remember you from Mr Hotaling's class. We called you "Little Miss Perfect". You used to remind him when he forgot to give us homework.'

Carter looked at Esme in astonishment. He laughed out loud.

Self-doubt weakened Esme's resolve, but she stood firm. A rule was a rule was a rule. At last, Arnold surrendered. He left his skateboard in the hallway. Esme stepped aside.

Carter tried the phone on the desk. 'No dialling tone,' he said. 'It's dead.'

Arnold sidled up to a row of new iMacs, dropped his pack on to a chair and started punching keys on one of them. He read the message on the screen aloud: '*Sorry, we have failed to connect to the Internet. Please try again.*'

He tried again, and again on different Macs. Nothing worked. 'That's strange,' he said. 'Wi-fi's out.'

Esme drifted towards the main windows, which offered a view of a small interior courtyard. She watched as crows alighted on the ground, one after the other. The black birds seemed agitated. They screeched and nipped at each other with sharp beaks. Fog hung in the air, as thick as soup.

'We could smash one of these windows,' Carter suggested. He picked up a chair, as if ready to hurl it.

'Dude, hold up!' Arnold said. 'Let's think about this a minute. The chains were put on *from the inside*, right? Somebody has to be in the building.'

'A night caretaker!' Carter agreed.

'Yeah, he probably didn't realize we were here,' Arnold reasoned. 'Nobody saw me come in, I know that much.'

Esme now counted thirty-seven crows — cawing, calling, screeching in high-pitched shrieks. It gave her a nervous feeling, as if the world had somehow gone wrong. 'Guys, come look at all these crows.'

'Um, no,' Carter replied. He turned and led the way out the door in search of the night caretaker. Arnold followed at his heels. Esme cast one last worried look out the window, sighed, and hurried after the boys.

They explored the dark, empty corridors until they stopped at a stairwell that led to the basement.

'I've been in this school for five years, but I've never seen these stairs before,' Arnold said.

Esme had no memory of seeing the stairway either. 'It's bizarre. I don't think—'

'What's the big deal?' Carter interrupted. 'It's a stairway. So what?'

A faint

**TAP-
TAP-
TAPPING**

came from below. It was followed by a rumbling, hacking cough. A cold draught rose from below and brushed up against Esme's legs like a cat. She shivered, as if touched by something evil.

Carter took a couple of wary steps downstairs, then stopped. Perhaps he felt the same chill in his bones. He looked up to Arnold and Esme, who remained rooted where they were. 'You coming?'

LIGHTS FLICKER
AND DIE

The stairs led to a metal-plated door. Behind it, Esme heard what she imagined to be the shuffling of boots, the jingling of keys, and a man sitting heavily in a chair. Carter knocked twice and, receiving no reply, pushed the door open.

An ancient man sat in the corner of the room at a grey metal desk. He stared at his visitors through red-rimmed eyes. His skin

was greyish-yellow, and his sunken, narrow cheeks gave off a skeletal appearance. Thin hair grew from his otherwise bare skull in wisps, like odd tufts of white grass. He wore blue workingman's trousers and a red flannel shirt.

He looked half dead, and Esme stifled a gasp at the sight of him.

The ancient man did not appear happy to see three students appear in his small, cramped office. He held a glass jar in one hand, and a fork in the other. He stabbed at a blood-red cube of meat from the jar and pushed it past his lips. He never moved his eyes from the uninvited guests.

'Venison,' he spat with a gruff voice. He speared another cube of meat and held it before his face. 'Deer meat. Kill it and butcher it myself. Care for a taste?'

No one accepted his offer.

'Didn't think so.' He chomped on the bloody flesh. A trickle of blood dribbled down his chin.

'Are you the guy who locked us in?' Carter finally spoke up.

The ancient man leaned back in his chair, reached to his belt, and splashed an enormous key ring on the desk. There had to be fifty keys of every size and shape.

'Are you going to tell us which one?' Carter asked.

The ancient man wiped the grease from his lips with the back of a sleeve. 'No,' he replied.

'Excuse me?' Esme asked.

'You don't want to go out there,' the night caretaker said. 'Not tonight, no.' He rose painfully and shuffled towards the heavy door, which he shut behind them with a firm hand.

Arnold grew alarmed. '*Ha!* Well, yeah.

I'm not sure you understand, Mr . . .'

'Van Der Klemp,' the old man said.

'Mr Van Der Klemp,' Arnold repeated. He helplessly pointed a thumb towards the ceiling. 'We accidentally got locked in the school, see, and . . .'

The old man didn't seem to be listening. He rubbed a large hand to his stubbled chin, noted the time on his wristwatch, and closed his eyes as if waiting for something to pass. He counted in a dry whisper, 'Three, two, one.'

The lights flickered and the room went dark.

THE MYSTERIOUS
MR VAN DER KLEMP

Esme shuddered. Carter reached for her arm, pulling her near. Arnold started muttering, 'Um, yo, guys? I'm like, not into being here right now with this *super-freaky* old guy and—'

'Silence,' Van Der Klemp hushed them. 'Wait for it.'

In the next moment, a battered generator kicked on. It clanged noisily in the corner until achieving a steady drone. Then the lights came back on, though dimmer than before.

'My backup generator.' Van Der Klemp smiled. He leaned his frail body against the desk, dabbed a handkerchief to his mouth, and coughed into it.

It left red dots of blood.

'Please, I have to get home,' Esme said.

'Not tonight,' Van Der Klemp replied darkly. 'It is too dangerous.'

The kids exchanged worried glances.

The night caretaker continued. 'You will wait until morning light. It is your only hope.'

'*Okaaaaay*,' Carter replied. He looked to Esme and Arnold. Gave a slight nod. Then he moved, fast. Carter snatched the keys off the desk. He bounced on his toes, ready for action. 'Listen, we are outta here. I'm borrowing your keys. And we're going home.'

The ancient man did not move. 'Unwise,' he stated. There was a trace of sorrow in his eyes. 'They already gather outside.'

'Come on, guys. I'm not listening to this guy,' Carter ordered. Following Carter's lead, they flew up the stairs, feet barely touching the ground. The old man did not try to stop them. The three students had nearly reached the library when Arnold slowed to a halt. 'Hold on, I've got to catch my breath,' he said. 'Besides, I left my backpack in there.'

Arnold went into the library for his backpack, while Esme sagged to the floor. Carter was still energized. He paced the hallway, pumping his fists. 'What a fruitcake!' he shouted. 'Can you believe that guy? Crazy as a loon – and creepy too!'

'I feel like I've seen him before,' Esme said.

'From school?' Carter asked.

'No, that's not it.' Esme tried to recall where she'd seen Van Der Klemp's face before. She drew a blank, as if a memory had been wiped clean.

'Yeah, I know what you mean,' Carter said. 'He seemed familiar to me too.' He rattled the heavy set of keys. 'One of these babies is going to get us out of school free, so we might as well get started. I don't want to be here in case Van Der Klemp starts creeping around.'

'Guys?' Arnold called from the library. 'You better come see this. Now.'

5

WALKERS IN THE MIST

'What?' Carter snapped, annoyed. 'We don't have time to mess around.'

'I'm serious!' Arnold said. There was urgency in his voice. And fear.

Arnold stood by a window at the far end of the library, from which vantage point he could observe the grounds behind the school. Through the mist, he could see the football pitch and basketball courts, the swing set and monkey bars, and the climbing frame that looked like an old pirate ship.

The wind was still. Not a leaf stirred. High above, a full moon appeared like a cloudy eye that stared, unblinking, through the mist.

'I wanted to check outside,' Arnold told them. 'After what that old guy said about, you know, it being dangerous.'

'Yeah, so?' Carter asked.

'Take a look,' Arnold said.

Esme gazed out the window. 'It's hard to see anything.'

'There!' Carter put a hand on Esme's back and pointed with his free hand.

As Esme's eyes adjusted to the darkness, she began to make out shapes moving across the grounds. Men and women dressed in clothing from olden times and others in tattered rags, all drifting aimlessly through the school playground.

A murder of crows flapped and bickered

near the figures, landing on heads and shoulders. None of the dark shapes seemed to mind.

'Their clothes seem so old-fashioned,' Esme said. 'Like they dressed up for a fancy party or a dance or—'

'A funeral,' Carter said.

Arnold hesitated, uncertain. 'Those people don't seem normal.' His breath smelt like spearmint gum. He cracked the gum loudly and chewed.

'*Nooooope*,' Carter agreed.

Could this be real?

Esme saw, or *thought* she saw, through the fog, a crow peck at the face of one of the figures. Again and again, the black scavenger plucked at the man's eyes.

Yet he shuffled along as if he was just a sad, pathetic scarecrow in a cornfield. Couldn't even scare away a crow.

THE FACE AT THE
WINDOW

'How come they're out there,' Carter wondered, 'just wandering around in the dark? It's freaky.'

No one dared to guess. But it didn't look right, they all felt it.

Dozens of figures ambled through the grounds. Listlessly, aimlessly, like school-children at recess without the energy to play. Some wore puffy dresses, others were dressed in suits and ties. They walked with arms at their sides, heads pitched forward, as if led by their noses.

'They don't seem *awake*,' Carter said. 'Like they are sleepwalking or—'

'Zombies,' Arnold said.

Carter snickered, 'Zombies. Yeah, right.'

'The zombie bash,' Arnold muttered. He popped a fresh piece of gum into his mouth and cracked it loudly. *Pop*. A burst of spearmint sweetness floated from his lips.

The figure nearest to the building sniffed. He lurched forward from the right, moving with surprising swiftness. He, or it, passed not five feet from the window, head lolling in every direction. He lifted his nose to the sky and sniffed like a wolf on a mountaintop. He howled, an inhuman cry, and stood with his back to the window.

Then slowly, awkwardly, the creature

turned around. His face appeared normal, yet every muscle was lax, dull and unexpressive. There was no emotion in it. A face without anger or joy, happiness or sorrow.

Lifeless.

But it was the eyes that terrified Esme. One eye was rolled back into the man's head, so that only white showed. An empty cloud, unseeing. The other eye was missing entirely, just an empty socket and a trail of blood.

Catching a scent of spearmint, the zombie's nose wrinkled. He drew a step closer. And let out another moan from deep inside his body, a pitiful sound of longing and pain and great hunger.

OOOOOAAAAANNNN, OOOOOAAAAANNNN.

Two hands shot out with lightning speed,

thundering against the plexiglas window.

BOOM, KA-BOOM!

The pane shook from floor to ceiling, but didn't shatter.

Arnold leaped back, stumbling against a table. Carter quickly pulled Esme away from the window.

'I – I . . .' Esme stammered. She couldn't breathe, couldn't think, couldn't talk. Her heart hammered in her chest.

'Shh,' Carter said. He whispered with surprising calm and gentleness, 'Shh.' Softly into Esme's ear. 'Shh.'

He guided them farther away from the window.

Away from the thing with dead eyes.

CARTER GOES
FOR HELP

Half an hour later, they had a plan.

And Esme hated it.

'It's too dangerous,' she argued. She listed all the reasons why it was a terrible, horrible, stupid idea. 'We don't know what those zombies will do,' she concluded. 'You can't go out there.'

Carter stood with his arms crossed, half listening. His mind was made up. He glanced impatiently at Arnold, who was methodically trying key after key in an exit door at the north-west corner of the building.

'How you doing with that lock?'

'Working on it, dude,' Arnold replied.

Esme placed herself in front of Carter. 'This is crazy,' she reasoned. 'Somebody will come for us. We just need to sit tight.'

'We've already been over this,' Carter said. 'My parents don't know I'm here. Same with Arnold, same with you. We all came here without telling anybody.' He said the next words slowly, patiently, firmly: 'Nobody knows we're here.'

Carter began to pace. 'I don't want to stick around with that caretaker downstairs. Besides, I'm not like you,' he confided to Esme. 'I can't sit around and wait. I get this boxed-in feeling, like I'm claustrophobic, you know?'

'No, I *don't* know,' Esme pleaded.

The key slid into the padlock.

'Got it,' Arnold whispered.

He unwrapped the chain.

'I'll be careful,' Carter promised. 'No worries. I'll walk out nice and slow. Remember, I live only two blocks from here. Piece of cake.'

'Maybe we should go with you?' Esme offered.

Carter shook his head no.

'Wait a sec,' Arnold said. He pushed off on his skateboard and glided down the hall. Two minutes later, he was back again – this time, carrying a hockey stick. He tossed it to Carter, who caught it with one hand. 'You might need a weapon,' Arnold said. 'I found it in the gym closet.'

'Sweet,' Carter said, as he slashed the stick through the air like a ninja.

Esme peered into the night. 'There's a few of them wandering around. What do they want?' she asked.

Arnold sighed, rolled his eyes. 'Hello? Don't you play video games? *World of Warcraft? The Elder Scrolls? Dead Space?*'

Esme stared at him blankly.

Arnold flung his hands up in exasperation. 'I don't know why there's a bunch of zombies out there.' He pointed beyond the door. 'You want answers? Ask them!'

'Van Der Klemp knows,' Esme said.

Arnold looked at her thoughtfully. 'Maybe,' he admitted.

Esme struggled to form the question. 'Do you think maybe they don't want to hurt anybody?'

Arnold shrugged, then glanced at Carter. 'I wouldn't stop to take a poll,' he advised. 'You saw that guy outside the window. Mr

Dead Eyes? Pretty scary if you ask me.'

Esme stepped closer to Carter. 'Don't go,' she urged.

He moistened his lips, grinned and opened the door. In a pretty good imitation of the Terminator, he intoned, 'I'll be back.'

The door opened.

An odour drifted into the building. A smell of decay, dead leaves and rotten flesh. The odour floated down the hallways, clung like vines to clothes, wafted into nostrils. It was the unmistakable aroma of death.

The door shut.

And Carter was gone.

OOOOOAAAAANNNN, OOOOOAAAAANNNN

For a few minutes, it seemed like the plan might actually work. Then the crows came. And things went very, very wrong.

As he'd promised, Carter stepped out into the mist with supreme calm. Cool as a lake. It was foggy, but he could still see about thirty feet in any direction. He gave a thumbs-up to the two worried faces that stood vigil at the door.

It's all good.

A crow landed near his foot and cawed noisily. Then another, and another. Carter stepped cautiously, not wishing to disturb the birds. He noticed a dark figure ahead and veered away from it.

'CAW-CAW!' Carter looked up to see a crow dive-bombing from above, talons out. The black bird hit Carter's head at full force, *wham*, and tore into his scalp.

'Ow, *shoot*!' Carter cursed. He staggered back a step, dazed, and waited for the dizziness to pass. Carter tenderly probed the injury with his fingers. His scalp was torn. Under a loose flap of skin, his flesh felt like raw hamburger. It was wet.

He checked his fingers. Blood. Lots of it.

OOOOOAAAAANNNN,
OOOOOAAAAANNNN.

The moans came, louder and louder, from every direction. As if the creatures were calling to each other. Now, more shapes appeared in the distance, moving towards him. *It's the blood*, Carter thought. *They smell it.*

His hands tightened around the field-hockey stick.

Esme called from the door. 'Carter! Carter! Come back!' she yelled.

He considered making a mad dash for home, weaving through the slow-moving bodies. But there were more of them now, arriving from all over, and in growing numbers. He returned to the school door.

But it didn't open.

'Guys?' he whispered. 'Let me in.'

In her panic, Esme tried to help Arnold with the key ring. It fell to the floor.

Carter slammed on the door with an open

palm. 'Kind of in a hurry out here,' he urged.

'Which key is it?' Esme screamed, frantically searching through the set. She was nearly blind with fright.

'Silver, square-shaped,' Arnold said.

A filthy, blackened hand with long fingernails reached out to Carter. He turned and sliced the stick through the air. *Thud*, it hit something. The hand fell to the ground.

'I gotta go!' Carter screamed. 'Meet me by the front doors!'

And he took off, zigging left, zagging right, spinning and slashing with the stick as he ran.

Faster. And faster.

Into the night of the zombies.

9

'THEY'RE COMING!'

Esme tossed the key ring to Arnold. He rocketed down the hallway on his skateboard. In seconds, Arnold was hunched by the front doors, feeding key after key into the lock.

'Come on, come on,' he urged.

Esme stood in the main lobby, a frayed bundle of nerves. She bit her lip, sucked on loose strands of hair, searched for any sign of Carter. Nothing. 'Something must have happened,' she worried. 'He should be here by now.'

Arnold kept working his way through the keys. One by one.

Carter appeared out of nowhere, running at full speed. He slammed into the door. 'Open up!' he cried. 'Now!'

He still clutched the field-hockey stick in one hand, but it had been broken in half.

'Arnold!' Esme screamed.

'I'm trying!' Arnold shouted back.

Carter pounded at the door. His chest heaved, and Esme saw, for the first time, pure terror in his face.

A hand plucked the key ring from Arnold's fingers. 'I believe these are mine,' Van Der Klemp said.

All eyes turned to the ancient man. The night caretaker held the keys high in front of his face. He fingered the keys, as if counting the beads on a rosary. 'Hmmm,' he murmured. 'Where are you? Where . . . are . . . you?'

Carter cried out as he pounded on the door,

'THEY'RE COMING!'

'Ah, yes!' Van Der Klemp whistled. Humming softly, he selected a key, inserted it into the lock, and turned. **CLICK**. It opened. Arnold and Esme unwound the huge chain from the handle . . . Carter pushed . . . and the door flew open!

In the span between two heartbeats, Carter slammed the door shut behind him. *Whew*.

Carter looked from one face to the other: Arnold, Esme and Van Der Klemp. After a few moments of stunned quiet, Carter reared back his head and laughed – a wild, unhinged whoop of relief and joy: 'I've *never* been so happy to be in *school* in my life!'

Esme wrapped her arms around Carter, squeezed him tight, then quickly pulled back. Arnold pumped a fist in the air. Carter was back. Van Der Klemp did not celebrate. He simply wrapped the chain back around the handles, pulling it tight. He closed the lock and returned the key ring back to its familiar place on his belt.

'You came to help us,' Esme said.

He waved a hand as if swatting away a fly.

'Why?' Esme asked.

The ancient man looked into the mist. 'I am the night caretaker,' he said, as if that explained everything.

'You *knew* this was going to happen,' Esme said. There was a new tone of anger in her voice. 'You warned us. You told us they were gathering outside.'

Van Der Klemp coughed into his soggy, red-tinged handkerchief.

Esme picked up Carter's splintered hockey stick from the floor. It was a sharp, dangerous weapon in her hands. A spear. 'Tell us everything you know,' Esme warned, 'or else.'

THE UNDEAD CANNOT BE STOPPED

Van Der Klemp stared long and hard at Esme. A resigned smile crossed his face. He turned to the others, who stood shoulder to shoulder, defiantly watching the old man. Finally, the night caretaker nodded.

'First thing, we need to stop this boy's bleeding,' Van Der Klemp said. 'Then we'll eat. You'll need your strength. And then . . . we'll talk.'

The moment Van Der Klemp mentioned food, they realized no one had eaten since lunch. It was now past nine o'clock. So they raided the teachers' lounge – a room legendary for its supply of cupcakes, sweets, treats, salads, sandwiches and assorted refreshments. Every student at Buzz Aldrin Primary knew that teachers ate like kings and queens, especially on Fridays.

Esme pulled a plastic container of brownies from the refrigerator. The group hadn't realized how hungry they were until they saw the food arranged on the table. 'Brownies with peanut butter cups!' Esme announced.

'I don't know, Esme,' Arnold teased, buzzing from sugar. 'This *might* be against the rules, and we know how much you *looooove* rules. Isn't that right . . . Little Miss Perfect?'

He grinned at her.

Carter sat leaning on an elbow, gauze pressed against his wound. He laughed softly.

Esme blushed, embarrassed. 'Well, I guess sometimes rules are meant to be broken,' Esme said, popping a brownie into her mouth.

She slid the rest across the table. For the next few minutes, they wolfed down food like it was a competition: who could pig out the most? Finally, Esme turned to Van Der Klemp and said, simply, 'So?'

All eyes turned to the night caretaker.

'The curse began when we – when *they* – built this school nearly one hundred and twenty years ago,' Van Der Klemp said. 'It was the perfect spot, a clear meadow on a hill. But there was one inconvenience.'

'There's an old photograph of it in the display case,' Esme confirmed.

Van Der Klemp nodded. 'That picture was

taken one hundred and twenty-six years ago.'

'You said there was an inconvenience,' Carter prodded.

'There was an old, abandoned graveyard near where the playground is now. Long story short: the graves were disturbed.' Van Der Klemp paused to suck on a tooth. 'It is a very, very bad idea to wake the dead.'

'Wait. What?' Carter said.

'This has happened before,' Van Der Klemp said. 'The dead rise every eighteen years to haunt the grounds for one horrible night. And always, the world forgets.'

Carter leaned back in his chair, frowning. 'That's crazy. You can't keep something like that a secret. It would be all over the Internet.'

The old man seemed exhausted. 'I speak the truth,' he shrugged. 'Believe what you wish.'

'I left bodies out there,' Carter said. 'People will know.'

'It will all be washed away,' the night caretaker said. 'The crows feast even now. Repairs are made, wounds will heal, memories will be scrubbed clean. Come tomorrow, if we reach tomorrow, none of you will remember the events of this night.'

'We'll forget?' Esme asked with a catch in her voice. Somehow, the thought of forgetting, of her memory wiped clean, frightened Esme more than anything. It would be like having parts of her life erased.

'Those zombies out there—' Arnold began.

'They are the sleepers that should never have been awakened,' the man said.

'So, what do we do now?' Esme asked. 'Can we fight them?'

Van Der Klemp shook his head. 'They

can be slowed, perhaps. But you cannot harm those creatures. The undead cannot be stopped.' He plucked a stray grey hair from an ear, studied it for a moment, flicked it away. 'The plan is simple. Stay alive until dawn. At sunrise, the spell breaks.'

'THEY WILL COME'

They decided to make camp in the library. Van Der Klemp called it 'defensible', noting that the large room had three exit doors. They agreed to keep the lights off and speak only in whispers. Do nothing that might attract attention.

Carter sat by a window to scan the playground outside. Van Der Klemp stood nearby.

'It's quiet,' Carter observed.

'For now,' the caretaker grunted.

'Do you think they will try to get inside?'

Van Der Klemp stole a glance at Esme and Arnold, who sat at a table across the room. He nodded. 'Yes, they will come. Remember that if things get bad, head to the roof. It's the last, best place.'

Across the room, Esme sat hunched at a table, writing furiously.

'What are you doing?' Arnold asked.

'I wrote it down, everything that's happened so far, all the details,' Esme said. 'I don't want to forget.' She plucked a black permanent marker from a coffee cup. She took Arnold's arm and scribbled in his palm:

VAN DER KLEMP ROCKS!

Arnold laughed. For a brief moment, they forgot about the danger outside. Later, Esme made two copies of her story, and solemnly gave one each to Carter and Arnold. 'Keep it safe,' she said. '*Remember.*'

As the hours crept past, the unthinkable became possible. Arnold stretched, Esme yawned. Even Carter felt his head loll and his thoughts grow fuzzy. Van Der Klemp told them to sleep. They huddled close on beanbags in the centre of the room for comfort as much as for protection.

The night caretaker took the first watch.

Time passed.

Creatures gathered in the night.

OOOOOAAAAANNNN,
OOOOOAAAAANNNN.

Carter's eyes snapped open.

OOOOOAAAAANNNN, OOOOOAAAAANNNN.

He sat up, his eyes adjusting to the dark.

Van Der Klemp snored softly. He had passed out in a chair.

Arnold also slept.

But Esme was gone.

Carter heard footsteps in the hallway. The squeak and groan of a door swinging open, banging shut. *Click*. A light switch flicked on. *She's in the bathroom*, he thought.

And then he smelt them, the zombies.

An odour of evil had entered the building, bitter and sour. It came like smoke, like fire, swirling and circling and searching through the rooms of the school.

It came like a warning, an alarm.

They are coming.

In that eerie silence, Carter could feel the blood push through his veins. He sensed the nerve endings of his fingertips, felt the air that passed from his lips. He waited, and hoped.

Arnold turned in his sleep, whispered, 'No, no.'

Just a dream . . . a nightmare.

CRASH!

A loud crack erupted, like a gunshot.

It was the sound of a window shattering, a thousand shards of glass falling to the floor, echoing in a tiled room.

The next thing he heard was Esme's scream — it was loud enough to wake the dead.

AND THEY CAME

Things happened quickly, a haze of events, shouts and screams and wild terror.

Esme burst out of the bathroom, the door flung wide. She was ashen-faced, followed by three dark figures who had broken through the glass window inside. Their bodies were stiff and convulsive – they moved in fits and jerks – but they were not slow. Their eyes were clouded white, unseeing.

They're blind, Carter realized.

OOOOOAAAAANNNN, the creatures moaned. The smell of death trailed them like a shadow.

Carter and Arnold stood, frozen in fear. Esme scrambled towards them, frantic, trembling. They stood together in shock, too stunned to move. Not one living soul stirred. The horror was too immense, too overwhelming.

More windows crashed, more noises came from down the hall.

Van Der Klemp pushed forward past Carter, clutching a mop crossways. 'Go,' he spat. 'Don't look back. Just run. Get to the roof!'

'But—'

'Arrrrr!' Van Der Klemp roared a thunderous cry, and he plunged forward to battle the undead.

They did not look back. Carter took Esme's hand, and they all ran.

Down the corridors, past the lobby . . .

'In here, the gym,' Carter said. 'They're blind. Maybe we can hide.'

'They can smell us,' Arnold argued.

More zombies filled the hallway.

Arnold hurried to the sports supply closet, where earlier he had found the hockey stick. He tossed makeshift weapons to Carter and Esme, outfitting his companions like some bizarre army in a future war game. They listened to the shuffling of feet, the rising hum of animal groans:

OOOOOAAAAANNNN, OOOOOAAAAANNNN.

Carter saw a hatch on the ceiling with a pull cord. 'Esme, climb up and open that hatch. We'll hold them off.'

'I can't—'

But there was no time. The zombies followed their trail like hounds, and had reached the entranceway. Carter swung his stick in wide, swooshing arcs. Arnold stood by a huge basket of baseballs and fired them at the heads of the oncoming zombies.

ZIIIINNNGGG! BOINK! CRACK! THWACK!

Skulls exploded. Zombies staggered and fell like bowling pins.

But they kept coming, and kept coming.

Too many, too many.

Up Esme climbed, up to the top of the raised seating at the back of the gym. *Can't* was not an option. She strained for the cord. She grasped it. Down, she fell with a painful thud, and then down the hatch came . . .

a ladder unfolding to the floor.

'Up, up, up!' Carter cried.

They crawled and scrambled and climbed. Grey, dead hands clawed at their feet, but the three kids somehow escaped to the roof, and slammed the hatch shut.

SUNRISE

They lay sprawled on the flat roof, panting, dazed, and exhausted.

Safe.

Esme sat up, looked around. She was bruised and battered and thrilled to be alive.

Mist hung in the air. It was still dark, still full of gloom. The roof was empty. There was an air-conditioning vent, some random pipes, a door and . . .

A door?

'Guys? Where's that door go?' Esme asked.

At that moment, the door splintered open. **OOOOOAAAAANNNN**, the zombies moaned.

They would not stop.

They could not *be* stopped.

And so they poured on to the roof like a deathless, unyielding flood.

Carter, Arnold and Esme stood in a trembling knot. They huddled close, waiting. They inched towards the edge of the building, looked down. It was too far to jump.

'I'm frightened,' Esme whispered.

'Shh,' Carter whispered. 'Be brave.'

A subtle change in light caused Esme to turn and face the east.

'Look,' she said.

The dawn's first slant of light appeared over the horizon. It blazed like a flaming arrow across the sky.

In that instant, the spell broke, just as Van Der Klemp had said it would. The zombies evaporated into dust and ash. The mist cleared in a *whoosh*, as if sucked from the sky. And so began a new day.

STRANGERS AT SCHOOL

On Monday morning, hundreds of students spilt out of buses in front of Buzz Aldrin Primary.

It was clean and beautiful. No broken windows, just a few crows on the lush, green lawn. A normal school on a typical Monday.

Esme Millstein paused outside the building. She filled her lungs with fresh, crisp, cold air. She had several pages folded neatly in her back pocket. They contained a haunting, amazing, impossible story. *Could it be true?*

Esme didn't know. She couldn't be sure. She didn't even remember writing it.

'Coming through!' a voice called. It was a boy on a skateboard, wearing a baseball cap screwed on sideways. He lightly bumped Esme as he zoomed towards the front doors. Esme remembered the boy from Mr Hotaling's class. *Arnold Chang.*

'Watch it,' Esme called after him.

The boy stepped off the skateboard. He paused to look at Esme. There was something in his eyes – a look of recognition passed between them. He smiled at Esme, opened his palm, and held it up for her to read:

VAN DER KLEMP ROCKS

'I can't wash it off,' he said.

Van Der Klemp. The words were in Esme's

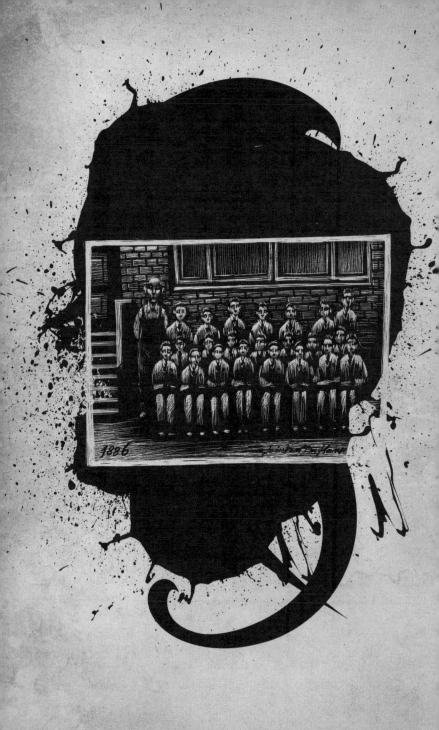

own handwriting. She had put it there – just as she had written the same name in her story.

Images from Friday night flickered in her mind. She remembered everything.

Inside the school, Esme noticed Carter Novack standing in front of the display case by the main office. He studied an old, black-and-white school photograph. It was a group shot with students, teachers, even the caretaking staff.

'What are you looking at?' Esme asked Carter. Carter stared at the girl, perhaps seeing her for the very first time. He pointed at the old caretaker in the photo. He had dark bags under his eyes. Thin tufts of hair grew out of his balding skull. He had crooked teeth and a strange, wary smile. The date of the photograph was stamped on the lower left corner: 1886.

'I feel like I met him somewhere before.

But that's not possible, right?' Carter said.

Esme pointed to a caption. 'Third row, left . . .' she read. 'Joris Van Der Klemp, caretaker.'

The bell rang. It was time to go. Esme did not wish to be late.

Carter grabbed Esme's sleeve. 'I remember now,' he said. 'I remember you. I remember all of it!'

'Me too,' Esme said.

And she smiled, even as a cold chill entered the building and made her shiver.

SO WE SAY FAREWELL TO CARTER, ARNOLD AND ESME. THREE STUDENTS WHO SHARED A NIGHT THEY'LL NEVER FORGET. THEY REMEMBER, THANKS TO WORDS WRITTEN IN THE EERIE SILENCE OF A DARKENED LIBRARY.

AND WHAT, WE WONDER, BECAME OF MR VAN DER KLEMP? NO ONE CAN SAY. BUT NEXT TIME YOU FIND YOURSELF ALONE IN THE HALLS OF SCHOOL, PERHAPS CLOSE TO DUSK, BE SURE YOU DON'T GET LOCKED INSIDE. IT COULD MAKE FOR AN AWFULLY LONG NIGHT.

LOOKING FOR MORE
THRILLS AND CHILLS?

DON'T MISS THE FOURTH

SCARY TALES

BOOK . . .

JAMES PRELLER
NIGHTMARELAND
SCARY TALES

Illustrated by IACOPO BRUNO

AARON WHEELER JUST GOT A STRANGE NEW VIDEO GAME CALLED NIGHTMARELAND. IT SUCKS AARON RIGHT IN.

BUT THAT'S NOT UNUSUAL. AARON COULD PLAY VIDEO GAMES ALL DAY. THE REAL WORLD JUST FADES AWAY.

THIS TIME, AARON IS WHISKED AWAY TO AN EMPTY GRAVEYARD. HE FINDS HIMSELF ALL ALONE, CAUGHT IN A SNOWSTORM. A HOWL COMES FROM THE NEARBY WOODS.

HOOOOOWL!

IT IS THE CRY OF WOLVES. AND THERE IS NO WAY OUT.

FANGS GLEAMING IN THE MOONLIGHT

'Aaron? I'm talking to you.'

Aaron blinked, looked up, and saw Addy beside him. He pulled the headset off his head.

'I'm going upstairs. Do you need anything before I disappear into my textbook?'

He shook his head.

'Are you OK?' Addy asked. 'You seem a little out of it.'

Aaron kept his eyes fixed on the television screen. A part of him felt like it was in that graveyard.

'Maybe you should take a break,' Addy suggested. 'Go outside, get some fresh air?'

'No, I want to do this.'

That was the end of the conversation.

Aaron felt a powerful connection to the figure in the video game as he moved through the desolate graveyard. It was as if Aaron could imagine exactly what it felt like to be in that place.

It was as if . . .

No, it couldn't be.

He was at home. Safe and sound. Sitting in the corner of an L-shaped sofa. Snug as a bug. A bowl of cereal at his side. Dry, no milk, no spoon, the way he liked it.

Aaron touched the tip of his nose. It was damp and cold. He glanced at the end of his finger. He watched a solitary snowflake melt away.

How could that be possible?

—〰—

With the controller in his hands, Aaron became the figure in the snow.

Walking in the graveyard, he shivered. Aaron blew warm air on his cold fingers. It didn't help. His legs felt heavy pushing through the thick snowfall. He continued on towards pale, yellow lights in the far distance. An old castle, perhaps. Not too far. He'd arrive in ten minutes, cold but happy, grateful for a warm fire. Ready for the next test in his adventure.

Tall trees moaned in Aaron's ears. Wind whistled through bare branches. The long limbs swayed like the arms of a great and groaning creature. The snow fell harder now, heavier.

He pulled the thick robe tight around his shoulders. Aaron focused on the lights ahead of him. He'd played enough video games to know that's where he needed to be.

Aaron had to find shelter, fast.

He became aware of movement amidst the trees. A dance of shadows. Black shapes shivered in the silence, loping from dark to dark, obscured by the swirling snow, hidden by tree trunks and shadows. The cold leaked into Aaron's bones. His toes hurt. The dry snow crunched beneath his feet and he walked to that rhythm.

Crunch, crunch. *Pause*. Crunch-CRUNCH.

Aaron knew he was being watched. He felt the pressure of eyes, like icy hands on his back. There was something out there.

A threat. He felt vulnerable in the graveyard. Nowhere to run, nowhere to hide. Now the clouds shifted and moonlight shone upon the frozen ground. Aaron could make out names on the tombstones. *Barrett*, *Shaw*, *Glassman*. It comforted him to read the names. But in the dark woods to Aaron's left and right, everything remained unknown – shades of grey, shadows of black. The trees formed tall, dark, vertical lines. The rest was nothingness, as empty as an abandoned warehouse.

He glimpsed the shadows that moved soundlessly amidst the trees, melting into the dark.

They loped on four paws.

Like dogs.

Like wolves.

Aaron saw their eyes, silver slivers of light, staring at him, waiting.

When he moved – slowly, cautiously – the

eyes of the wolves moved with him. They meant him great harm. He knew it in his bones.

Aaron knew that the wolves meant to follow him and then . . . they would attack as a pack from all sides.

He slipped and fell. Aaron quickly rose, steadying himself. He spun around fearfully, hands lifted in defence.

There was nothing there.

Aaron was alone in the clearing of a valley, surrounded by woods.

Just a boy in the snow.

Except he was being hunted by wolves.

SCARY TALES

JAMES PRELLER
is an extremely experienced
author of mystery-horror
stories for children. He lives
in New York with his wife,
three kids, two cats and a
golden labradoodle
called Daisy.

IACOPO BRUNO
is a graphic artist and
illustrator who lives in Italy.

OUR BOOKS ARE FRIENDS FOR LIFE.